Little, Brown and Company

Hachette Book Group
1290 Avenue of the Americas, New York, NY 10104
Visit us at lb-kids.com

Little, Brown and Company is a division of Hachette Book Group, Inc. The Little, Brown name and logo are trademarks of Hachette Book Group, Inc.

The publisher is not responsible for websites (or their content) that are not owned by the publisher.

First Edition: February 2015

Library of Congress Control Number: 2014953637

ISBN 978-0-316-28353-3

10 9 8 7 6 5 4 3 2 1

RRD-C

Printed in the United States of America

Disney FAIRIES

Tinker Bell
AND THE LEGEND OF THE
NEVERBEAST

The Chapter Book

Adapted by Stacia Deutsch

Ⓛ Ⓑ

LITTLE, BROWN AND COMPANY
New York   Boston

Chapter One

I ridessa was gathering light beams near the Pixie Dust Tree in Pixie Hollow when a strange green glow passed over her. She paused in the field of flowers to watch it. The light moved past Tinker Bell in Tinker's Nook and caught the attention of an owl, who swiveled his head to follow the comet's trail.

Scribble, a reading-talent sparrowman, looked out a telescope at the strange green light flashing across the sky. He jotted notes on some parchment, never taking one eye away from the viewfinder. The green light hovered over a small cave before disappearing inside.

Deep inside that cave, where the fairies

couldn't see, the green light ended its fantastic journey. The green glow intensified and suddenly...an enormous glowing eye blinked open.

The next morning in Pixie Hollow, Fawn was enjoying the perfect day. She flew quickly, skimming water with dragonflies and joyfully greeting a family of bears before blasting into the sky to join a flock of birds. She enjoyed the warm sun on her face and the wind in her hair, then curled into a cannonball and rocketed back down to the earth.

As she dropped through the tree canopy, she grabbed a leaf and used it like a parachute to soar the rest of the way down, swinging past Never Land's magnificent animals and the fairies who were caring for them.

Fawn loved her job with the animals. She landed near a groundhog who was refusing to dig a hole. It only took Fawn a few minutes to solve the problem. She tackled the groundhog and popped underground with him. An instant later, they'd created a burrow together.

Next, Fawn raced two pillbugs to the bottom of the hill. Then she landed on the back of a bunny, who playfully tossed her into the air with its powerful legs. She nudged a nervous baby bird out of his nest, catching him as he first fell, then flew. The bird smiled at Fawn as he went to join the others, and she soared off toward the sky, breaking through the treetops.

When Fawn got home, Tink was there already. She'd made Fawn a cart out of a large blueberry basket mounted on thread spool wheels.

"Oh, Tink! It's perfect!" Fawn exclaimed.

"Just like you ordered, Fawn, one extra-large wagon....But what's it for? I mean, why all the mystery?" Tink asked.

Fawn didn't tell Tink the reason she needed the contraption. She began to wheel the basket away.

Tink said, "You're up to something."

Fawn shrugged. "Who, me? Never."

"Yep, you definitely are. I know that look. I invented that look." Tink asked seriously, "What's the wagon for?"

Fawn gave up. "Okay, okay, just...try not to scream, deal?" She swung open the door to her house. Inside was a baby hawk.

Tink couldn't believe her eyes. "You— You have a...*hawk*! Fawn! Hawks *eat* fairies!"

Fawn nodded. "Oh, adult hawks, yes— Hannah's still technically a baby. That whole must-eat-fairy urge hasn't *quite* kicked in yet," Fawn said. "She had a bad wing, but I fixed her up, and now..."

Hannah flapped her injured wing, knocking over everything, including Fawn and Tink.

"Wing's all better!" Fawn cheered.

"You can't have a hawk in Pixie Hollow! What if the scouts find out?" Tink asked.

"That's where the blueberry wagon comes in!" Fawn explained. "We just have to get

Hannah out to where she belongs without causing...you know...widespread panic."

Fawn grinned. "Let's go!"

Tink sighed. She really didn't want to help, but she knew Fawn needed her.

A few minutes later, they'd loaded Hannah into the cart and covered her with blueberries.

As they moved the cart through the Animal Den, the animals started to act strange. A bear nervously scooted into his hole. Two pillbugs turned into balls and rolled away. A pair of mice lowered their heads to hide.

"Fawn?" Tink was getting nervous.

"Just keep smiling," Fawn replied through clenched teeth. At that moment, the cart rolled over a bump in the ground and a berry bounced off. Tink quickly put it back in place. "See, Tink? I told you this would work...." Fawn paused when she noticed pixie dust falling from the sky above. "Pixie dust?"

It was Rosetta. "There you are! We've been looking for you all morning!"

Iridessa, Vidia, and Silvermist were with her.

"Hey, did you guys see that comet last night?" Iridessa asked.

"No, but did you see that big green ball of light that flew by?" Silvermist replied.

Rosetta changed the subject. "What's with the berries?"

Fawn hummed. "Just bringing them to the forest. For the animals."

"Don't berries come *from* the forest?" Vidia wondered.

Fawn said quickly, "Not this particular variety, which is, um...extra berry-full-licious-tastic!"

Silvermist was excited. "Yum! Can we help?"

Fawn brushed her away. "No. We're fine...."

"Oh, for goodness' sake, there's an easier way to do this." Without permission, Rosetta sprinkled pixie dust on the berries. The berries began to rise....

"Wait. No—" Fawn tried to stop her.

"It's called helping," Rosetta said. "A simple 'thank you' would suffice."

The dusted berries kept lifting rapidly into the air....

"What are you all staring at?" Rosetta asked the others.

The girls all backed off, wide-eyed. Every animal and fairy in the Animal Den turned to stare. Then Hannah chirped.

The fairies screamed! Animals and fairies were running and shouting, trying to get away from Hannah. Hannah was scared from all the screaming. She flapped her wings and squawked.

Nearby, three adult hawks heard the noise. They hurried to the Animal Den.

A fairy on lookout sounded the alarm. "It's a hawk! Run!" The scout raised her spyglass and saw Hannah while the adult hawks buzzed by.

Chapter Two

Queen Clarion was in a meeting with Scribble. He was telling the queen about his latest research. He had a lot of charts and reference materials to explain the mysterious comet. "That comet is an astronomical puzzle to be sure," he was saying, "but careful observation and application of the scientific process will allow us, or rather, me, to determine exactly—"

Suddenly, scout warning sounds blared through the castle. Queen Clarion turned to the window to see the animal fairies flitting around in a panic. The large hawks were overhead, preparing to dive....

"HAWWWWK!" a fairy screamed.

9

The first hawk swooped low and tried to grab a baby beaver. The beaver was fast, and the hawk missed. He swirled around, looking for another animal to snatch.

Hannah quickly abandoned the blueberry basket and took off into the air.

"HANNAH! Hannah, stop! Come back!" Fawn went after Hannah, while Iridessa and Silvermist worked on a game plan down below.

"Everyone, get inside!" Iridessa shouted as a large hawk chased the fairies in all directions.

"IRIDESSA!!" Silvermist shrieked as a hawk headed directly toward her friend.

Iridessa flew as fast as she could, but it wasn't fast enough. The hawk opened its razor-sharp talons and...

"Oh no!" Silvermist gasped.

WHOOSH.

Iridessa thought she was safe until something grabbed her from behind. But it wasn't the hawk!

"Nyx?" Iridessa asked quizzically.

Nyx was the leader of the elite scout fairies.

She was cool, confident, and very fast. After taking Iridessa to a knothole, she faced the first hawk with a porcupine needle spear.

When the hawk backed away, Nyx gathered her four scout mates, Fury, Di, Shade, and Chase. They soared through the sky and fell into perfect formation behind Nyx.

The hawk moved on from Iridessa and chased baby animals through the Animal Den. He found another helpless fairy to attack, but suddenly Chase and Di flew past his beak, distracting him.

Fury came in, jumping to launch herself off Nyx's spear toward a second hawk circling above. Midair, she lassoed her rope through his beak before landing on his back and riding him like a horse. She turned around just as Chase and Di led the first hawk directly into his path!

The two hawks collided and then flew away together.

Fawn looked around panicked. "HANNAH? HANNAH!"

As she was searching the trees, the third hawk came in fast and close and tried to grab her in his talons. Fawn barely escaped.

Below her, Tinker Bell was getting the animals into a space to hide. "Go! Get inside! Hurry, go!" A baby bear got stuck in the small hole, and Tink tried pushing his backside. "Come on!"

Suddenly, Tink felt a shadow fall over her. She turned to find the large hawk hovering above her. She was trapped. The hawk opened his beak wide—

WHACK!

Nyx swooped in at the last second and wedged her spear into his beak and propped it open. Then Chase dove in front of him and threw a weighted rope around his legs. Shade and Fury swooped in and helped drive the last adult hawk away.

With the three adult hawks gone, Chase trapped Hannah in a net.

"Wait!" Fawn rushed forward. "Everybody

calm down! I promise, she doesn't even like the taste of scout fairy."

"Babies are such picky eaters," Silvermist whispered to Rosetta.

Nyx stepped forward. "Get away from the hawk, Fawn. Let us handle this."

"There's nothing to handle, Nyx," Fawn said.

"I said stand down, Fawn!" Nyx ordered.

Just then, Queen Clarion arrived. "Is everyone all right?"

"Yes, Queen Clarion—this time," Nyx reported. "But how am I supposed to keep us safe if Fawn keeps bringing dangerous animals into Pixie Hollow? Last time it was rats and a snake!"

Fawn corrected her. "Actually last time it was a vampire bat—"

"Fawn's just got a big heart, that's all," Tinker Bell cut in. "Hannah needed her help."

Fawn squeezed Hannah's face and said, "Does this look like the face of a dangerous predator to you?" No one agreed. "C'mon, back me up, guys," Fawn begged.

The animal fairies said nothing. Queen Clarion moved in close to Fawn. "Fawn..." she began.

Fawn sighed. "I know, I know, Nyx is right—I've done this once or twice...or several times... before."

"Yes..." the queen began again.

"Maybe harboring a baby hawk...wasn't the best idea," Fawn said.

"Fawn, I know you," added Queen Clarion. "You've always let your heart guide you, which is admirable, but—"

Cutting her off, Fawn finished the thought. "But...I also need to listen with my head."

The queen nodded.

"Next time, I promise I will," Fawn said as she moved quietly toward the net. "Well, Hannah-Banana, I'd say come back and visit, but probably best to keep this a long-distance thing. Now let's give that wing a try." Fawn yanked away the net and Hannah flew free.

Chapter Three

The next day, Fawn was back at work. "Good morning, students! Beautiful day for a fresh start, don't ya think?" Her students were three baby bunnies named Calista, Nico, and Paige. "All right then, let's see that hopping."

The bunnies began to hop around as Fawn playfully tossed them a couple of berries. "Nice work, Nico! Perfection, Paige!" Calista needed some more practice. "Ooh, Calista—remember, it's hopping, not walking."

Calista looked at her teacher.

Fawn said, "What, haven't you heard? I'm strictly by the book now. Yep, we're talking model citizen all the way. Looking for the definition of responsibility? Look no further than this girl!"

Fawn was interrupted by a loud moan echoing through the forest. Fawn's head swiveled.

"Well, that was...interesting."

Fawn turned back to her class to find that Nico and Paige had already run away. And before Fawn could speak, Calista darted off, too.

"Now that's hopping," Fawn said, watching her go.

But she couldn't forget about the noise. Cautiously, Fawn followed it. "What was that?" She looked down the path toward the mysterious sound. "Hello?"

When she pushed through a bush into an area of broken branches, she saw a rock with fur stuck under it. Fawn bent down, examining a patch of the odd fur on the ground. Then she noticed that she was actually standing in a gigantic paw print!

Bravely, she followed the trail of prints through the forest. Up ahead, she heard another distant groan of pain.

Following the sound, Fawn entered into a clearing and stopped.

The landscape was strange, moonlike, stripped of vegetation. The ground was pockmarked and cratered. In the center of this clearing was a strange cave with jagged rocks around the entrance—as if something pushed its way out from underground.

Fawn slowly crossed and peeked into the blackness of the cave. "C'mon, Fawn, listen to your head. Heart gets you in trouble; head is your friend," she said to herself. "And yet, head is making me talk to myself...out loud...in the forest." She started to back away. "No, no, no, model citizen—starting first thing tomorrow."

And with that, Fawn flew forward and disappeared into the darkness.

Slowly, she moved deeper and deeper into the cave. The passage was strange and twisted. She ducked under an overhang, and as she stood, she gasped, staring ahead with a look of wonder.

A strange, hairless tail snaked around a corner.

Fawn followed it. She went deeper into the cave each time she saw the shadow move.

"What are you?" she asked, trying to get a better look.

All she could see of the creature was a paw the size of an elephant's foot. And in that paw, there was a painful thorn.

Fawn took a steadying breath, flew straight to the thorn, and pulled on it with all her might. It wouldn't budge.

Just then, a pair of menacing green eyes blinked open and the beast stood up, revealing himself. He was as big as a buffalo, with a thick snout and a jutting jaw full of razor-sharp teeth. There were strange swirls covering his matted fur.

Fawn was terrified, but she tried to keep her cool, unsure what was going to happen next. "Okay, think—territorial, possibly carnivorous... unspeakably big. What to do? What to do?" She dropped to the ground. "Play dead!"

Then she changed her mind. "No, no—

freeze." Fawn popped back up and froze in place.

Another idea. "No, the opposite—make myself look big." She waved her arms, growled, and tried to appear larger than life. The beast stared at her.

"RRRRROOOOOOOAAAAAARRRRRRRR!!!!"

The earth-shaking blast went out like a shock wave, bending everything in its path as it tore across the landscape!

The cave spit Fawn out.

She crash-landed in the Thorny Thicket. The smart thing to do was leave, but then the beast moaned again. This time the wounded creature sounded even more in pain than before. She had to help.

Fawn didn't know it yet, but she'd discovered the NeverBeast.

At the scout tower, Fury saw the sound wave rumbling through the forest. "What was that?"

Nyx glared toward the sound. "Trouble..."

In the Animal Den, the baby birds were chirping.
Fury called out to the animal fairy who was
conducting the birds in their song. "Did you
hear it?"

"Hear what?" the fairy asked.

"The roar," Fury said. "Did you hear the roar?"

The fairy pulled cotton out of her ears. "Sorry,
did you say something?"

Chase asked a fairy named Buck, who was
working with the squirrels, about the roar.

"You bet I heard it," he told her. He turned to
the squirrels and said, "A little faster. Visualize
the acorn right in front of you."

Chase said, "Excellent! What was it?"

Buck shrugged. "No idea. But let me know as
soon as you find out."

An animal fairy named Morgan was coaching
a baby skunk how to spray. "Gently now: to the
left! The other left!"

Nyx dropped in front of her, pulled the

skunk's tail down, then asked Morgan, "That roar..."

"This morning?" She'd heard it.

"What was it?" Nyx asked.

"Oh, I don't know. I don't specialize in roars. Now, grunts and growls on the other hand—" Morgan was going to explain more, but Nyx cut her off.

"Who would know?" Nyx asked.

"Well, if it came from anything big—" Morgan said.

"Loud—" Buck said.

"Scary—" the bird fairy added.

"—and dangerous. Try..." Morgan was about to say the name when Nyx finished for her.

"Fawn." Nyx frowned. She had to find Fawn.

Fawn was hiding behind a rock, watching the beast. He came out of the cave, limping. She whooshed past him. He grunted before moving forward again.

She continued to follow the beast, darting back and forth and taking cover when necessary. She hid under a mushroom, then behind a tree, until the beast stopped at a pile of large rocks.

Balancing on his hind legs, the beast dug at a large red boulder. It was stuck. He dug harder, but his paw slipped, and he fell forward—right onto the injured paw.

He roared in pain.

"Hmmm..." Fawn was thinking of a way to help.

The beast smelled her scent and turned. She quickly escaped into a tree.

The beast sorted through stones, putting aside gray ones and choosing the red ones.

Fawn knew what she could do: She pushed a red boulder forward. "Come on, big guy, over here." The beast followed it.

As the beast walked over to the rock, Fawn released a branch attached to a rope that pulled the boulder up into the air. The beast got up onto his back legs, trying to reach the dangling rock.

This was Fawn's chance. She took a deep breath and flew right at him. As he chomped down on the rock with his teeth, she landed on his paw, grabbed the thorn, and pulled it free.

Fawn fell to the ground and rolled away, but her foot got caught in the rope, which was now pinned under the large rock. The beast saw her. She tugged at the knots, trying to get free, but the beast stood over her, snorting hot breath.

He opened his mouth. Fawn stared at his dagger teeth. "Wait! I was only trying to help!" she said, panicking.

The beast lowered his head and chomped down...on the rock. He picked up the boulder in his teeth and carried it away.

"Huh? Hmmm." Fawn watched him lick his paw and stomp on the ground. It looked like he was agreeing to let her live. Fawn stood up and took a deep breath. "Huh, those thick forelimbs are ideal for digging." Then she tried to convince herself to leave, saying, "Nope. No, no, no, no, you're all fixed up, so—off I go!"

The beast went back to collecting rocks. But Fawn didn't leave. She continued to study him. "And that massive jaw is perfect for supporting those heavy rocks." She stepped into his way. He glared at her and she moved aside. "Y'know, it's like you're a cross between Didelphis Marsupialis and Bison Occidentalis..."

The beast then spit out a twig of snodgrass sap.

"...that spits. I don't know what that's about." She sighed.

The beast added another rock to the pile. He was clearly building something.

"And I don't know what *that's* about," she muttered.

The beast wrapped his tail around a branch and hung upside down, using his tongue to pick up a red rock from a deep cavern below.

Fawn hung by her knees on an opposite branch nearby, thoroughly confused, yet fascinated. "I really don't know what that's about. What are you building?" She paused, then told herself, "Y'know, it is my job as an animal fairy to understand and study animals. And the queen did say I should listen to my head."

The beast didn't reply. Fawn was forming a plan.

"You've convinced me. I'll do it," she told herself. "For the queen."

The beast kept moving rocks.

"Now, stay here, okay? I'll be right back. I just need to get my stuff. Don't go anywhere! Just stay." She flew off, but popped right back. "Stay."

Chapter Four

Fawn rushed home to gather tools. When she arrived, Nyx was standing in her doorway.

"I've been looking everywhere for you." Nyx leaned her spear against the door frame and stepped inside. "So, where ya been? Off hiding a hippo?"

"Yep, he's bunking with the bobcat," Fawn replied.

"Did you hear that roar this morning?" Nyx asked her.

Fawn paused. "Can you describe the roar in question? What kind of roar was it?"

"The loud, hair-raising, monstrous kind," Nyx told her.

Fawn began piling tools in Nyx's arms. "Animals make all kinds of roars. I mean, you've got your growls, howls, whoops, hollers, shrieks, and rumbles. Was it...like this?" She shrieked like a cat.

"No," Nyx said. "A roar."

"Oh. Sort of like a..." Fawn trumpeted like an elephant.

"No."

Fawn whined like a hyena.

"No."

Fawn howled like a wolf.

"No."

Fawn shrieked like a chimp.

"Fawn—" Nyx started.

Fawn jumped in. "Yeah, if you hear that one, run. Would you hand me that?" She pointed to a ball of twine.

"Look. This thing might be a threat to Pixie Hollow." Nyx shoved the tools back into Fawn's arms. "If you find out what made that roar, I need to know." When Fawn didn't reply, Nyx added, "Are we clear?"

"What will you do if you find it?" Fawn asked.

Nyx picked up her spear, spun it, and headed to the door. "My job," she said.

Fawn frowned, then added the ball of twine to her pile, muttering to herself, "And I'll do mine."

Back outside the NeverBeast's cave, the creature was still hard at work sorting stones. Fawn landed in one of his giant footprints and measured its width by walking across it.

After that, she snuck in from behind, dropping a measuring tape over his ear, checking his size. She made a note on her clipboard.

Suddenly Fawn shrieked as the ground rumbled. The beast was rolling another rock.

Fawn slid under him to snip off a piece of his fur. She ducked in a hole to hide, but when the beast rolled a rock on top of her hole, she was trapped inside. "Hello?" she called out.

She found a way to free herself and began

working on sewing clumps of the beast's fur together to make a beast costume. With a mighty roar, she jumped out of the brush.

The beast ignored her.

When night fell, Fawn created a bed from brush and sticks, just like the beast was doing, but the beast rolled a rock over her bed, crushing it.

The next day, Fawn began stomping in a circle, exactly like the beast.

When the beast rolled a giant boulder with his snout. Fawn did the same with a small pebble and her nose.

The beast was building a mighty tower. Fawn added her pebble to the rock pile, but the beast carelessly flicked it away.

Fawn sighed. She simply wanted to understand.

She sat down and tried to draw a picture of the beast. He turned away from her. Fawn's drawing was a mess. The day was getting away from her, and she hadn't learned much about him yet.

Day turned to night. Fawn flew near the beast's head and suddenly his eyes lit up when she glided past. Her glowing pixie dust trail caught his attention and he looked up, captivated. It was a breakthrough! Fawn grinned and took a note.

As she wrote in her notebook, the NeverBeast abruptly nudged her with his giant nose. Fawn and the beast had connected! His expression was soft and gentle. She smiled back at him.

Fawn began sprinkling pixie dust on top of a boulder. The rock began to levitate, and she gracefully placed the rock on top of the beast's pile. He allowed her contribution to remain.

Hours passed, Fawn and the beast's tower continued to grow, but Fawn was getting tired. This time, when she got into her makeshift bed, the beast walked around it. Fawn yawned and fell fast asleep.

The next morning, the beast nudged Fawn awake. She muttered, "I cleaned out the skunk pen yesterday...." Then Fawn realized where she was. The beast was right in front of her! "Oh! Good morning!" she said happily.

In the distance was the finished tower. It was a giant structure, curving into the sky, tapering to a point out of view. It looked dangerous, sharp, and yet beautiful.

"Looks like somebody's a night owl," Fawn said. She circled the tower, examining it. "What is this?" The beast suddenly grabbed Fawn and put her on top of his head. "Oh. Okay." Fawn went along for the ride, asking questions as they went. "So, where to? Anywhere but scout headquarters...Look, if I'm gonna cover for you, I need to know—what's the tower for? This one beaver I know, Bob—great guy—he makes dams big enough to store food for three winters!"

The beast didn't answer, so she went on. "And of course marmots build these terrific burrows out of rock piles for hibernation. And then you've got your northern orioles and those hanging nests of theirs—talk about brilliant! But I'm thinking you're not storing food. Or preparing for hibernation. Or nesting." The beast grunted as if to agree.

"Seriously, what's the tower for?" Fawn asked.

The beast snarled.

"Well, you don't have to be so gruff about it." She paused, thinking about what she'd said. "That's it. Gruff. Yep, Gruff suits you to a—"

The beast, now Gruff, whipped his tail around, yanking Fawn off his back. She looked around. They were now in the Summer Forest. Gruff immediately began to stomp the ground for a foundation.

"Guess we're building another one," Fawn said.

Gruff dug out a boulder.

Fawn was about to help when suddenly she had an idea. She flew up next to him. "But before we start, I was just thinking: Why not enjoy yourself a bit while you work?"

Gruff grunted.

"Just hear me out. No reason I should have

all the fun with the pixie dust." She showed him how she could sprinkle dust on the boulder he was rolling. It floated up. "Come on!"

Gruff found he could easily push the boulder with his tail. He grunted.

"Now we're talking." Fawn raised a few rocks.

Gruff used a snout, tail, paw combo to sail them into formation. It was so much easier this way. Fawn flew back and forth, setting up rocks for Gruff. They all landed in the right spots.

Fawn pretended she was a sports announcer. "Fairies and sparrowmen, presenting the three-time defending champion of the Pixie Hollow Games tower-building event—the amazing, incomparable Gruff!" Fawn cheered. "Will he hold off this year's pint-sized yet feisty challenger?"

Gruff's nostrils flared as he took the rock challenge and slammed three floating rocks into the pile.

"And he nails it!" Fawn announced.

Until...the boulders hit the pile with so much force, the tower fell over.

"But it's too much!" Fawn claimed victory. The rocks she flung to the pile stayed put. "The fairy wins! The fairy—"

An instant later, Fawn's smile faded as she realized Gruff's rocks had gone over a cliff and fallen onto Sunflower Meadow below. "Oh nooooo..."

Down in the meadow, the garden fairies had just finished blooming the last sunflower.

"And done. This may be our best spring yet..." a fairy was saying when Fawn's voice boomed from above.

"INCOMING!!!"

The garden fairies looked up. In a flash, a field of sunflowers and several nurseries were destroyed. The garden fairies barely made it out alive.

Nyx and her scouts came to examine the damage.

"The boulders came from that direction?" Nyx pointed up at the cliff above.

"Affirmative," Fury said.

A garden fairy said, "If Fawn hadn't shouted that warning, we'd be flatter than a pumpkin seed."

Nyx paused. "Fawn?" She glanced up at the top of the hill.

From the ledge, Fawn saw Nyx looking at her. She turned and said, "Hey, Gruff, I think it's time we make like a tree and get..." But Gruff was gone.

"Oh," Fawn said, wondering where he went.

Chapter Five

Fawn raced through the forest, following Gruff's prints. "Come on, Gruff! Where are you?"

She was moving so fast, she ran right into him. He ignored her as he gathered more red rocks.

"Gruff! No time for rock collecting! You gotta get outta here. GRUFF!"

In the distance, Nyx and the scouts came over the ridge to find Gruff's pile of rocks above Sunflower Meadow.

Fury noticed a mangled shrub in the background. "Nyx..." She called the leader.

Nyx examined the leaves. "Snodgrass." Then,

using her tracking skills, Nyx followed a trail of soft paw prints. She signaled her crew. "Knock it out with the nightshade powder!"

Fawn caught up with Gruff. She needed to get him away from the scouts.

Desperate, Fawn flew in front of him and did a loopty-loop, shaking pixie dust everywhere. "Okay, new game, Gruff. It's called 'Chase the Fairy'!" She took off and Gruff sprinted after her. "Now follow me!"

Fury and Chase spotted Gruff and Fawn speeding through the forest.

Chase whistled to Fury and she pulled three pouches of nightshade powder from her bag and tossed them in the air. Then Chase launched an arrow at the pouches, which burst, but the wind shifted and the smoke made all the scout fairies sleepy. They fell out of the sky.

Nyx bolted forward, expertly dodging the flying branches and leaves. She blasted out of the forest and pulled up at the edge of a cliff. There was no sign of Fawn or the beast anywhere.

Directly below Nyx, Fawn hid Gruff in the camouflage of a rock wall. She sighed as Nyx moved off in another direction. "That's my big, furry monster...." she whispered to Gruff. "Maybe it's time to make proper introductions."

Nyx returned to Pixie Hollow and entered the Book Nook.

Scribble was there, absorbed in his research.

Nyx interrupted. "Get me every animal volume you have in here immediately—"

"Please. I'm in the middle of a high-level, special royal project. Oh, did I say royal? Oops, top secret—" Scribble put her off until he saw who was there. He didn't think there was a lovelier fairy than Nyx. "Oh. Hello. How may I help you?"

Nyx repeated her demand, and Scribble got to work immediately on piling up the animal books, carrying so many at a time they made him look as if he had muscles. "And this is just the *As*. Y'know, books are a workout for the brain...and the biceps."

Knowing she needed him, Nyx tried not to glare. She flipped through each book, not finding what she needed. Scribble kept bringing more texts to her. When she reached the *Zs*, she buried her head in her hands wearily.

The whole time Nyx was looking, Scribble had been talking to her, but she wasn't listening. Then she heard him say, "And so I said, 'Listen, QC–Clar, most sparrowmen couldn't stomach this kind of pressure, but then again, I'm not most sparrowmen. And besides, that mysterious green comet isn't going to analyze itself.'"

Nyx looked around the room as she listened, her eyes drawn to a piece of parchment on Scribble's bulletin board. On it, there was a beast drawn with a distinctive tail and fur markings, and a comet drawn above the creature's head.

In a flash, Nyx flew across the room, swiping the fragment off the board.

"Hey!" Scribble shouted.

Nyx got in his face. "Tell me everything you know about this. Everything."

"Over dinner?" he asked hopefully. She didn't blink. "Oh, okay. I see. I've misread this situation entirely, haven't I?" He sighed to himself. "We'll always have the As."

That evening, Fawn gathered her friends near Gruff's Summer Tower.

"First, thank you guys so much for meeting me here. I'm sure you're wondering what this is about."

Tink, Vidia, Silvermist, Iridessa, and Rosetta were all there. Rosetta was already dressed for bed.

Fawn told them, "So, as you know, I really learned my lesson about being smarter when it comes to dangerous animals."

The girls all nodded.

"We know."

"We're really proud of you."

"Oh, honey, you are doing great."

"Yeah, you're doing really good."

"I never thought you'd make it this far," Vidia said.

"However—" Fawn began.

"And here we go." Vidia rolled her eyes.

"Fawn..." Tink braced herself.

Fawn took a deep breath and moved aside. "Ladies, say hello to Gruff."

The NeverBeast was hanging upside down in the tree behind Fawn. He dropped down from the tree branch.

Iridessa fainted.

"What. Is. That?" Rosetta asked.

Fawn shrugged. "I actually don't know. I've never seen any animal like him before. Ever."

"What does he eat?" Tink asked.

"Not fairies," Fawn said.

"Oh, well, that's a relief!" Silvermist said.

"So I'm gonna take him to the queen and show her he's harmless," Fawn told them. "Then I'll tell her how he destroyed Sunflower Meadow.

Well, how *I* destroyed it. You know what, maybe it was both of us." The NeverBeast grunted and Fawn corrected herself. "It was an accident, okay?"

Gruff agreed and went back to work.

"And what do you call that?" Vidia asked about the tower.

"Again, I don't exactly know...but I'm working on it!" Fawn said.

Rosetta frowned. "I'm hearing a lot of 'I don't knows' in this conversation."

"Umm...uncertainty makes me uncomfortable," Iridessa complained.

"C'mon, have I ever put you guys in danger?" Fawn asked, seriously.

Rosetta answered honestly. "Uhh, yeah."

Silvermist said, "Yep."

Iridessa said, "Frequently. Remember Peter the Porcupine? I still can't sit up straight."

Vidia waited a beat before saying, *"HAWWWWWWWWK!"* She was reminding them about Hannah, just to prove a point.

"Oh, yeah." Fawn remembered it all. "The point is—I want to do the responsible thing this time, just like I promised."

The girls looked at one another, then Tink turned to Fawn. "I'm guessing you already have a plan in mind?"

She did. "Operation Gruff-a-Go-Go."

A little while later, Fawn and the others had coated Gruff in pixie dust and flown him through the sky. Fawn sat on his head as the girls guided them toward the Pixie Dust Tree. Gruff landed softly.

Fawn hopped. "Open up, big guy!" She used his own spit to smooth his fur.

"Eww! My skin is gonna break out!" Rosetta shivered.

"Okay, so I'll go in and set the stage. Then on my signal, get him in position, and I'll bring her out," Fawn said, then whispered to Gruff, "Don't worry. She's gonna love you."

Fawn stepped away. "Here I go! Model citizen, all the way!"

The girls cheered her on. "Good luck! Be brave! You can do it, sugar!"

The girls watched Fawn as she entered the queen's chambers.

"She's doomed." Vidia sighed.

Fawn started speaking the minute she entered through the queen's door. "I've been thinking about what you said, which is why I'm here to tell you that—"

Clarion turned and Fawn saw that Nyx was there, too.

Fawn changed her mind about telling the queen. "I—uh—you know what? It can wait. I'll come back."

"Fawn, I'm glad you're here," Queen Clarion said.

"So am I..." Nyx grinned.

"Nyx has discovered a dangerous animal in Pixie Hollow. We could really use your expertise...." the queen began.

Outside the Pixie Dust Tree, Gruff was trying to get away from the girls and go to Fawn.

Tink peeked in the queen's window to see what was going on.

"Ugh, I am on the verge of perspiring over here. Do you see the signal?" Rosetta asked.

Fawn subtly gestured at the window, trying to tell Tink to take Gruff and leave.

But Tink didn't understand the hand motions.

Nyx explained, "I had my first direct sighting earlier today. This is no ordinary predator we're talking about. It's bigger and faster than anything we've ever seen. I combed through every animal text in the library, and came up empty. But it turns out, I was looking in the wrong place."

Tink flashed an "I don't understand" gesture to Fawn.

The moment Nyx and the queen looked away, Fawn exaggerated her gestures, until it looked like she was playing charades.

Nyx noticed her wild gesticulations, but Fawn

covered them up by pretending to do a dramatic
yawn.

Outside, Tink realized what was going on.
"Back to the forest!"

"What?" Iridessa asked.

"Mission abort!" Tink said. "Mission abort!"

Nyx made Fawn stay and listen as she told her
about the ancient parchment and its predictions.
"That comet that went by the
other night—it was here before...nine hundred
seventy-two years ago. And each time it passes,
it wakes the creature." She showed Fawn a paper
fragment that had a drawing of the beast on it.
"This is the NeverBeast. Once the comet brings it
out of hibernation, it starts building."

Another fragment showed Gruff's stone
towers.

"Four rock towers," Nyx said. "One in each
season of Pixie Hollow." She went on with
another picture. "Green clouds fill the sky. Then
the creature transforms and brings a lightning storm
so powerful, it consumes all of Pixie Hollow."

In the final drawing, lightning vibrated from the towers, destroying Pixie Hollow.

"If we don't act fast, this storm will destroy us all," Nyx said.

She pointed at the fragmented drawings, now pieced together to form a single ancient parchment: The Legend of the NeverBeast.

Chapter Six

Outside, Tink and the girls were doing their best to move Gruff. They pushed and pulled, but the beast was stubborn.

"Back home, please!" Tink said.

"C'mon, Gruff," Iridessa told him.

"Let's go," Rosetta tried.

"On three! One...two...*THREE—*" Tink counted.

As Vidia grabbed his ear, Gruff inhaled sharply, getting a whiff of Tink's dust, before exploding in a sneeze.

Nyx and Clarion turned at the sound. Fawn pretended it was her sneeze. "Phew. I should get that checked out." Then Fawn told the queen,

"Look, animals do not control the weather."

"*Ordinary* animals don't...." Nyx countered.

Fawn held up the drawing. "Furthermore, this creature with the horns and the bat wings...An animal that big couldn't possibly fly under his own power."

She glanced out the window to see Gruff darting back and forth, out of control, as her friends chased him around.

Nyx grabbed the parchment. "Either we capture the NeverBeast or life as we know it is over."

"Nyx, let's not do anything rash until we know more," the queen said. "See if you can locate the creature first."

"I just don't want innocent animals to get hurt," Fawn said.

"And I don't want innocent fairies to get hurt." Nyx turned to Fawn. "I'm not the enemy here."

The queen stepped between them. "I trust

50

you both to do what's right for Pixie Hollow."

Nyx stood straighter. Fawn tightened her jaw. They both were determined to do things their own way.

Outside the queen's chamber, Nyx's scouts waited.

"What's the word?" Fury asked her.

"We go after it at dawn," she said without hesitation.

That night, Gruff floated through the sky, pixie dust trailing behind him as he slowly descended.

Fawn caught up. "What happened?" she asked her friends. "You were supposed to get him out of there."

"We tried, sug," Rosetta told her. "Giant thing wouldn't budge."

"I think he didn't want to leave you," Tink said.

Fawn stroked the beast. "I missed you, too, Gruff."

Vidia interrupted. "Sorry to break—whatever this is—up. But what happened to doing the right thing?"

"Nyx got there first," Fawn reported.

"And...?" Iridessa asked.

Fawn flew up and sat on Gruff's nose. "Nyx found this harebrained legend about a creature called the NeverBeast who builds rock towers and shoots lightning to destroy Pixie Hollow, so now she thinks he's some kind of monster."

The girls' eyes widened.

"I know! Crazy, right?" Fawn said, but it was clear the girls believed Nyx.

Gruff landed, and Vidia began to back away. "Well, early day tomorrow."

"Oooh, am I tired!" Iridessa was leaving, too.

"Really? I'm wide-awake!" Silvermist missed the point.

Rosetta grabbed her, saying, "Bye-bye now."

Fawn shook her head at them. "C'mon, guys! You don't really think any of that stuff is true?"

But they did.

"It's just, I know he's not what they say he is," Fawn said.

"Even if you're right, it's not safe for him here," Tink said.

Fawn thought about Tink's words.

Nearby, Gruff was finishing building the tower in the Summer Forest. He put the last rock on and walked to his cave.

Fawn went along. She sat with the beast, staring up at the starry sky.

"Hey, big guy. Done for the day?"

He grunted.

She said, "Rest up, because first thing tomorrow, we're gonna find someplace great for you. Just until things settle down." Fawn leaned back, looking up at the sky. "Gruff, you see those stars over there? If you connect them, they make a monkey. See his tail?"

Gruff grunted.

"But if you turn it upside down, it's a swan. See?"

The beast watched as she traced patterns in the sky.

"That one's a squirrel. Oh, and over there, with the spikes? Hedgehog." She looked at him. "See it?"

Gruff grunted again.

"I knew you'd get it. You just have to know how to look." She flew up and sat down on his nose. "Imagine—you a monster. Of all the ridiculous ideas. I know they're wrong about you."

The NeverBeast snorted softly.

"They don't see what I see." Fawn closed her eyes and fell asleep.

A shooting star streaked across the sky. It was very peaceful. But, a moment later, green clouds began to gather in the distance.

Gruff opened his eyes and watched the sky.

At dawn, Fawn woke up, sensing that something was wrong. She was lying on her back in the dirt.

"Gruff? Gruff?" She looked around.

The beast was gone.

At scout headquarters, the team was getting ready. They put on armor, gloves, and wrist guards. They gathered bows and arrows, nightshade packs, and porcupine quills. They were ready for action.

Nyx flew to the balcony and the scouts followed. She paused and looked out at the green sky and declared, "It's starting."

All through Pixie Hollow, fairies were waking up to the strange glowing sky.

"What is that?" one said.

"It's so green," another replied.

"I've never seen anything like that," a third fairy remarked.

Tink noticed the crowd gathering to watch the sky. She looked up and discovered Nyx and the scouts crossing the green sky, carrying a large net with them.

She gasped. She had to warn Fawn.

"Gruff? Gruff? C'mon, Gruff. It's Chase the Fairy, not Run Away from Her." Fawn was busy searching for the NeverBeast.

"Fawn?" Tink shouted her name with urgency.

Fawn came out, and Tink quickly reported. "The scouts—they were geared up and moving fast. Please tell me you took him away already."

Fawn paused. "About that...I sort of... temporarily...misplaced him."

"You lost him?" Tink was stunned.

Fawn was still confident. "I got this. I just have to find him before the scouts do." She thought about it and realized where he'd gone. "Ah! He's gonna build two more towers. One in autumn, one in winter."

"I thought you said the legend wasn't real." Tink lowered her eyes.

"Technically, I said he's not what they think," Fawn clarified.

"But everything Nyx warned us about—it's happening. Just look at the green clouds, Fawn." Tink pointed up.

"Ehhhh...seafoam at best," Fawn replied with a laugh. Then she became serious. "Look, it doesn't matter what Nyx's legend says. All I know is, Gruff would never hurt us. Please, Tink, trust me."

Tink gave in. "I'll take winter." She started off.

Fawn stopped her. "Hey, Tink!" Tinker Bell turned. "Thanks."

Chapter Seven

Fawn raced through the Autumn Forest, bursting into a clearing—and screeched to a halt.

The tower there was done, but Gruff was gone.

The scouts arrived at the tower to find no one there.

Nyx studied the structure. "Just like the other two. Just like the drawing."

Fury kneeled at the edge of the woods and discovered a broken branch. Fresh sap remained on the raw break. She pointed to a trail of more snapped twigs.

"It's headed toward summer," Chase told the others.

The scouts took off, following the beast's trail.

The scouts continued to fly through the forest. From behind a tree, Fawn watched them fly toward the Summer Forest, then she took off in the opposite direction.

Nyx didn't go with the others. She stood by the rock tower, looking at a map of Pixie Hollow. She'd already drawn Xs for towers one and two in spring and summer. She made an X for tower three in autumn. She knew the next one had to be in winter.

On the other side of Pixie Hollow, Tink flew low over the Winter Woods snow.

"Gruff?" she called.

The green sky was all around her. Lightning sparks bounced off the rocks of a new tower.

"Gruff! There you are! We've been looking everywhere for you!" Tink said.

The NeverBeast rose from behind a snowbank,

but there was something different about him now. He was more intense. His nostrils flared.

He took a step toward Tink. She took a step back, saying, "Gruff, it's me, Tink. Fawn's friend. The scouts are coming for you! You have to hide."

It didn't seem like he recognized her.

Another strike of lightning zigzagged across the sky, followed by a huge crash of thunder. Tink was afraid.

She saw a bolt of lightning reflected in Gruff's eyes. Suddenly, he lunged at Tink, swatting her hard with his tail. Tinker Bell tumbled through the air. She hit the ground hard and crumpled into a heap.

Fawn arrived in the Winter Woods to find Tinker Bell unmoving on the ground. She rushed quickly to her. "Tink! Tink?" She turned to Gruff. "What did you do?"

Gruff growled.

A lightning bolt crackled in the sky. Right before Fawn's eyes, Gruff transformed.

Horns grew out of his head. A hump formed on his back. He was now exactly like the image from Nyx's parchment.

Fawn was horrified. "No!" Gruff was a monster.

She threw herself protectively over Tink until the thunder died down. When she glanced back up, Gruff was gone again.

Chapter Eight

A t the Fairy Urgent Care Medical Center,
Iridessa, Vidia, Silvermist, and Rosetta
huddled around Tink's bed.

Fawn stood in the doorway, feeling guilty, like
this was all her fault.

"Is she going to be okay?" Iridessa asked.

"She needs to rest," a healing fairy answered.
"Stay off her wings for a few days. She'll be all
right."

Rosetta said, "Oh, thank goodness."

Silvermist exclaimed, "That's a relief."

"Great news." Vidia was glad.

When Rosetta turned to say, "See, Fawn, she's
gonna be..."

Fawn wasn't there.

Fawn found the beast and moved in cautiously.
"Gruff?"

He turned around at the sound of her voice.

Fawn said, "Come down. I need to see you."
She reached out. "Gruff..."

Suddenly, a cuddlevine net launched through
the air and landed on Gruff.

Fawn looked terrified, but without warning,
the scouts leapt out from the bushes. It was an
ambush. Fawn moved out of the way and let the
scout fairies do their work.

Gruff bucked and kicked as the net dropped
over him. The cuddlevine cinched tight, dragging
him down to the ground.

"Stand firm!" Nyx told her troops.

The fairies tossed nightshade powder over the
beast.

Gruff made eye contact with Fawn and
tried to pull toward her. He stared at her with

a look of heartbreak and betrayal.

"Let's move out!" called Nyx. They poured pixie dust over Gruff so they could fly him out of the woods.

"You did the right thing," Nyx whispered to Fawn.

Fawn didn't think so. She walked away, sat down on a rock, and cried.

The fairies took Gruff to scout headquarters and tied him up.

"Whatever this is, it should have stopped by now," Fury said.

"Just stick to the plan," Nyx told her. "Immobilize the NeverBeast, and the storm disappears."

But that wasn't true. Outside, the sky continued to darken.

"Get everyone to cover until this blows over," Nyx ordered. "Get to the shelter—move! And secure the doors!" She went to stand in front of the NeverBeast. "Stop this! I order you—stop this now!" The towers crackled with electricity.

He didn't respond and a moment later, she took off, leaving a trail of pixie dust.

At the Urgent Care Center, Tink saw one of the megabolts through the window. "I have to find Fawn!" Tink announced in a panic.

But Fawn was already there. "Tink..."

"Fawn!" Tink was so happy to see her.

"It's over. He can't hurt you anymore," Fawn said.

Tinker Bell was confused. "Gruff?"

Fawn nodded slowly. "He's a monster."

"No, Fawn. He's my hero." Tink told Fawn what happened. "When I found him in winter, he was acting really strange." She explained how a lightning bolt zoomed across the sky, hitting a tree near Tink. The tree split and Gruff roared, then leapt, swatting the tree away with his mighty tail.

"He was protecting you." Fawn put her head in her hands. "And I betrayed him." She started toward the door.

"Where are you going?" Tink asked.

Fawn gave a small smile. "To do the right thing."

Silvermist and Tink went with Fawn to the scout headquarters.

They tried to let Gruff go, but the net wouldn't budge. Just then, Rosetta, Iridessa, and Vidia arrived. They shook pixie dust over the net.

"Thank you," Fawn said as the net rose.

"Go—take cover! C'mon, Gruff," Fawn said.

Gruff didn't seem to see her.

"Gruff?" Fawn was worried when lightning struck hard nearby. "Listen to me. You're having a reaction to the nightshade."

Gruff picked up her scent, but his eyes were clouded. He could, however, see the glow of her pixie dust.

"You can see my glow! Don't worry, Gruff. I'm gonna get you out of here." She reached out and rubbed his nose.

Lightning exploded through the sky.

Gruff roared and knocked Fawn away as a bolt of lightning struck him dead-on!

Chapter Nine

As the electricity hit Gruff, raw patches on his back began to expand and his jointed ribs unfolded. A spidery membrane stretched over the beast's back, between his shoulders, then unfurled into giant wings!

"Well, I did not see that coming," Rosetta said.

Taking a moment to think about what she was seeing, Fawn realized that Nyx had it backward. Gruff wasn't there to destroy them. He was there to save them!

"The towers—they draw in the lightning so he can collect it," Fawn exclaimed. "It's what he's been preparing for the whole time!"

Gruff grunted toward Fawn.

She told her friends, "We're going to the towers." Fawn knew she was right this time. "For once, my head and heart—they're actually telling me to do the same thing." Fawn went before Gruff to lead the way. "All right, big guy. Just follow my glow."

Gruff followed her blurry form. Just past the trees, Fawn saw the rock tower in the Autumn Forest. It was lit by lightning strikes.

Fawn was a little scared, but Gruff reassured her by bowing his head and going straight in toward the tower.

Suddenly, the lightning bounced off the tower and struck Gruff's horns. The light engulfed him until, with a great and mighty crack, the rock tower exploded.

After taking down this tower, the storm cleared from that area.

Gruff moved on to the next season area and the next tower. This time to the Winter Woods.

The lightning snapped off the tower and slammed into Gruff. Then, as with the first tower, it collapsed to the ground.

"Two down, two to go!" Fawn shouted.

Gruff went straight to the Summer Forest to take down the third tower.

When he was finished there, three streams of light, one from each of the towers he destroyed, were now flowing into him.

Fawn cheered him on. "One more, Gruff!" She led the way to the Spring Valley and the last tower.

Fawn and Gruff were about to finish the job, when, suddenly—

A giant pixie dust-coated boulder hit the tower at full force. The tower exploded, sending rocks hurtling through the air like missiles.

Beyond the collapsed tower, Nyx stood proudly.

"NO!" Fawn screamed.

WHAMMM!! Gruff crashed to the ground, skidded to a stop, and lost control of all the energy concentrated in his body.

Fawn rushed to the scout fairy and shouted, "Nyx! What are you doing?!"

"Saving Pixie Hollow," Nyx replied.

Fawn pointed at Gruff, who was struggling to get up. He was so weak. "No, *he* was saving Pixie Hollow."

The air crackled and Nyx's hair stood straight up on end.

"Nyx!" Fawn shrieked as one of the bolts headed directly toward her.

Nyx prepared for the impact, when suddenly Gruff appeared over her. He absorbed the lightning instead and saved her life.

Nyx was speechless.

"Nyx, we don't have much time." Nyx was staring at Gruff with new understanding. "Listen to me. Get out of here. Get everyone to safety."

Nyx took off, leaving Fawn to help Gruff with the lightning and the last tower.

Gruff hurried to start rebuilding the tower. He was rolling boulders into place, his vision still foggy. Lightning was everywhere.

"Gruff, it's too late." Fawn tilted her head. "How can we catch it all?"

Fawn looked at Gruff, who was looking up to the center of the storm.

They locked eyes, understanding what needed to be done.

"Follow me," Fawn said.

Gruff started to run, gaining speed. His wings flapped hard, beating the air—and then he was airborne. Fawn flew close to his ear so he could follow her glow.

Gruff took the lightning hits one after another. As they neared the storm's vortex, he grabbed Fawn with his tail and moved her behind him, then flapped hard, up and away from her to protect her. The fury of the storm emptied into Gruff's body.

Gruff blasted the lightning energy off with his wings, sending a shock wave of heat and light safely out to sea, into the void, far from Never Land.

In Pixie Hollow the fairies shielded their eyes from this explosion. No one spoke for a long time, until Iridessa asked Silvermist, "Can you see them?"

"There!" Silvermist pointed.

Two bodies tumbled from the sky.

"Fawn!" Tinker Bell shrieked.

The girls bolted into the air, racing to their friend. Nyx zoomed to their aid, too, calling to her scouts, "Help them!"

Silvermist and Iridessa carried Fawn gently to the ground.

Nyx and the scouts landed with Gruff.

As the beast hit the ground, he staggered to his feet, scorched and dazed. Gruff shook his back, and his wings crumbled into ash and blew away. The nightshade had worn off. He could now see clearly. He saw the fairies. And then he saw Fawn. She was hurt.

Chapter Ten

Gruff rushed over and circled Fawn. Tears welled up in his big eyes. He nuzzled Fawn's cheek and one last tiny current of static electricity squeezed out through his fur. It flowed from him into Fawn, wrapping around her body.

An instant later, Fawn's eyelids fluttered open.

"Hhhhuh...Gruff?" she asked on a whisper. Gruff grunted. "Hey. That's my big furry monster."

Gruff roared happily.

Fawn giggled and the crowd cheered.

"Gruff." Fawn hugged her friend.

Fawn gathered everyone together. It was time for a fresh reading of the NeverBeast parchment. Fawn had rewritten the story. "Every fairy should know the true story about the NeverBeast," she said. "He is the brave guardian of Pixie Hollow."

She held up a drawing of the NeverBeast. "He is our hero. And his name is...Gruff."

A few days later, Gruff was helping the fairies rebuild the animal nursery. It was just one of the many things he had done to help fix Pixie Hollow. Everyone loved having him around. After helping with a roof, Gruff yawned, which worried Fawn.

She lowered her ear to his chest to listen to his heart.

"Looks like he needs a nap," Iridessa said.

"A little rest'll perk him right up," Rosetta added, then asked, "Won't it, Fawn?"

Gruff sat down in the dirt, too tired to keep working.

"His work is done," Fawn explained to the others. "It's time for him to go back into hibernation."

Rosetta asked, "How long are we talking about? A month? A season?"

Vidia saw Fawn shake her head. "A year?"

Fawn tried not to cry when she told them, "More like a thousand years."

"But that means—" Silvermist started.

"We'll never see him again," Tink finished.

Fawn didn't say anything more to them. She flew up onto Gruff's nose, looking him in the eyes. "It's time...."

The fairies led Gruff through the woods, heading for home.

It was a beautiful, magical procession; the path was lit by orbs of moonlight captured by light fairies and hung from branches like lanterns.

When they reached the inner chamber of the cave, the girls gave Gruff gifts. Tink made him a comfy bed. Rosetta gave him a pillow. Silvermist added a freshwater spring. Iridessa gave him a nightlight. Vidia provided a gentle breeze.

Nyx also had a gift. But it wasn't something Gruff could touch or hold. She bowed in respect.

Fawn was last. "Hey, big guy. I won't see you again. But I know you'll always be there when we need you. I'm really gonna miss you." At last, she pulled back to gaze into his face. "I love you, Gruff."

He gazed back at her, also full of love. Then, slowly, his eyes started to close and Gruff drifted off to sleep with a happy smile.

Don't miss Tinker Bell
and the Disney fairies'
swashbuckling adventure
in *The Pirate Fairy*!

Chapter One

B eyond London, past the second star to the right and straight on 'til morning, lay the glistening hills of Never Land. Above the meadows of Pixie Hollow, graceful fairies flitted across the blue sky.

But not Zarina.

She walked into Sunflower Meadow, where Rosetta, Silvermist, and Iridessa were working together to grow a lush field of flowers. Each fairy has their own special talent, which tells what their tasks are.

"There we go," Rosetta said as she planted seeds. Silvermist watered the soil.

"Little bit of sun." Iridessa added her touch,

then, noticing her friend Zarina, she said, "Oh, look!"

Rosetta gazed up and, seeing that Zarina was traveling on foot instead of flying, remarked, "Hey, Zarina. Out of pixie dust again, sugar?"

Zarina shrugged. Her red hair glistened in the sunlight. "You know me, Rosetta."

"I could give you some tips on conserving your supply," Iridessa suggested.

"I may just take you up on that, Dessa," Zarina said as she hurried out of the garden.

Silvermist shook her head. "A dust-keeper fairy who's always out of pixie dust."

"Ironic, isn't it?" Rosetta replied.

Zarina walked quickly through animal-fairy headquarters, where Fawn was busy bathing a couple of baby birds.

"Lift that wing! Right there—nice!" Fawn said to the birds. "Okay. Rinse time. Time to dry." The birds moved past Fawn's cleaning station to where Vidia was drying them with a soft gust of wind.

Zarina scurried by.

"Hey, Z! Wings okay?" Fawn called out.

"Just enjoying a stroll, but thanks, Fawn! Nice wind, Vidia!" She hurried away.

"Thanks." Vidia looked up from the birdbath. Then she asked Fawn, "What's a *stroll*?"

Zarina could see the Pixie Dust Tree in the distance.

"Oh no!" At the sound of a whistle signaling the start of her shift at the Pixie Dust Depot, she picked up her pace and jogged the rest of the way.

After stamping her fairy card, Zarina entered the pixie dust distribution area and slid down a rope to the assembly line area. Her work smock had a large Z in the center of it. She slipped it on, blew the hair out of her eyes, and took her place in the distribution line without a moment to spare.

Terence the sparrow man—what male fairies are called—blew his kazoo, marking the start of the workday. The assembly line began to roll. Pixie dust swirled around a central vat, funneled down into barrels, and then dropped gently onto leaves, where the measuring dust-keepers made sure there was just the right amount.

Zarina's station came next. As each package went by, she leaned in and studied the contents before wrapping the leaves into neat dust-filled packages.

"Uh." The dust-keeper next to Zarina pointed at Zarina's bangs, which were now floating up thanks to the pixie dust she'd sprinkled on them.

Zarina considered her hair. "We put the dust in the bags, and the bags stay there, right? And yet, we sprinkle dust on top of something, and it floats." She put a pinch of dust on her ponytail. The hair rose up toward the sky.

Suddenly, everyone in the line paused, pixie dust packages in hand.

The dust-keeper said, "Well, that's just how pixie dust works."

While everyone else seemed to accept that answer, Zarina didn't. She asked, "Well, yes, I know, but *why* is the question...isn't it?"

No one answered.

"Know what I mean? Not even a little? Never once had the thought?" Zarina asked them.

The dust-keepers still stared at her blankly.

Fairy Gary, the head dust-keeper, entered the factory floor, along with his assistant, Terence.

"Good morning, dust-keepers!" Fairy Gary greeted everyone.

Zarina shook the pixie dust out of her hair and muttered, "Oh!"

"All right, let's see, on Blue Dust Duty today, we have..." Gary looked at Terence. "What were we on?"

Terence looked at his list. "Y."

"Ah yes, Yvette." Gary glanced around.

"Yvette's out for the day, Fairy Gary. Her dust-keeper elbow flared up again," a fairy reported.

"That's fantastic!" Zarina suddenly shouted, then softened. "I mean, poor, poor Yvette."

"Well, that brings us to—" Fairy Gary stared at the list.

Zarina pointed to the Z on her apron. "Z."

"Z," Fairy Gary echoed with a long sigh. "Zarina, you're up."

"Uh-oh," a dust-keeper muttered as Zarina left the assembly area with Fairy Gary.

Zarina followed Fairy Gary into the Blue Pixie Dust Vault.

"I mean, one day early. It's so exciting," Zarina said happily. She stopped talking as Gary opened a fancy chest with a secret combination lock.

"Six clicks to the right..." Zarina watched him carefully, reciting the code from memory.

"Yes," Gary said. "Thank you."

The lid slid open.

"Whoa," Zarina gasped.

Inside the chest was the super-rare, amazing, sparkling Blue Pixie Dust. Blue Dust strengthened the Pixie Dust Tree and helped the tree make enough golden pixie dust for all the fairies in Pixie Hollow.

With their daily ration of pixie dust, fairies could fly and make magic. Pixie dust was extremely important, and adding Blue Dust to the tree was a huge responsibility.

Zarina took the job seriously. She slowly collected blue flecks into a clear glass vial.

Fairy Gary watched her. "Careful now: After last time, I am sure I don't have to remind you just how potent and powerful this—"

"No touching. I promise," Zarina said.

"Attagirl. All right, then, exactly twenty-six specks," Gary reminded her.

"But why twenty-six?" Zarina asked.

Gary sighed. "And here we go...."

"Why not twenty-five? What would happen if we put in, say, twenty-seven?"

"Zarina, you're the most inquisitive fairy I've ever known." Gary changed his mind. "Correction: It's a tie. Let's just say you're the Tinker Bell of dust-keepers."

"Why do you say that like it's a bad thing?" Zarina asked.

"Because we don't work with twigs and acorn caps. We work with pixie dust. It's our lifeblood." He paused before reminding her, "There's no room for error."

Fairy Gary and Zarina entered the boughs of the Pixie Dust Tree. The tree glowed as it made golden pixie dust. Zarina could see that the usual trickle of pixie dust was slow and weak.

Zarina handed Fairy Gary the vial. Fairy Gary poured the dust into a beautiful wood-and-glass container, refilling the tree's well with the precious blue flakes.

"Blue Dust—one of nature's mightiest multipliers—takes the golden dust from a trickle to a roar...." Gary said.

Zarina stood behind Gary and watched as the Blue Dust dropped speck by speck into the golden dust. The stream of golden dust grew bigger and brighter than before, cascading in a waterfall down the side of the tree.

"No matter how many times I see it—just, wow!" Zarina said. She thought it was beautiful.

"Indeed," Gary agreed.

Zarina knew that Blue Pixie Dust was created when the light of the Blue Moon shone through a moonstone at exactly ninety degrees. That's why the Blue Dust was so rare and precious, but still, Zarina wondered about other possibilities.

She asked Gary, "But, if there's Blue Dust, why *can't* there be other colors?"

"Because there aren't," Gary answered.

"And maybe those other colors do other things. What if there was—I don't know— purple? What if there's pink?" Zarina asked.

Fairy Gary chuckled. "The day someone finds pink pixie dust is the day I trade in my kilt for trousers."

Zarina's eyes lit up. "Well, what if we don't find it? What if we *make* it?"

Fairy Gary looked at her in a serious way. "Listen carefully, Zarina: We do not tamper with pixie dust; it is far too powerful."

"But if we don't, we'll never fully understand what it's capable of," Zarina said.

"That is not our job. We're dust-keepers," Gary told her. "We nurture the dust, maintain it, measure it, package it, and distribute it. A beautiful tradition, day in, day out, passed from one generation to the next to the next to the next."

Fairy Gary continued, but Zarina wasn't listening. She'd taken off her bracelet and dipped it into the well of golden dust. She watched as it rose into the air, and then flicked it with her finger into the path of the Blue Pixie Dust.

The combination of Blue Dust and golden dust supercharged her bracelet! Like a torpedo, the bracelet shot up. It bounced around the tree, ping-ponging off the limbs of the tree until— WHACK—it hit Fairy Gary in the face.

"Oh no. Fairy Gary! Are you okay?" Zarina asked.

Gary grunted.

"Technically, I didn't touch it this time." Zarina frowned.

Gary simply took her bracelet away. He removed the empty Blue Dust vial from the tree receptacle and held it toward Zarina.

"The cap." He said it, and Zarina put the lid on the vial. Then Gary lectured her, "Let me be absolutely clear, Zarina: Dust-keepers are forbidden to tamper with pixie dust."

With that, he flew away, leaving Zarina alone at the tree.

Read more Disney Fairies adventures out now!